Magic Arthur

and the Giant

by Jan Slepian and Ann Seidler

illustrated by Richard E. Martin

Follett Publishing Company

Chicago

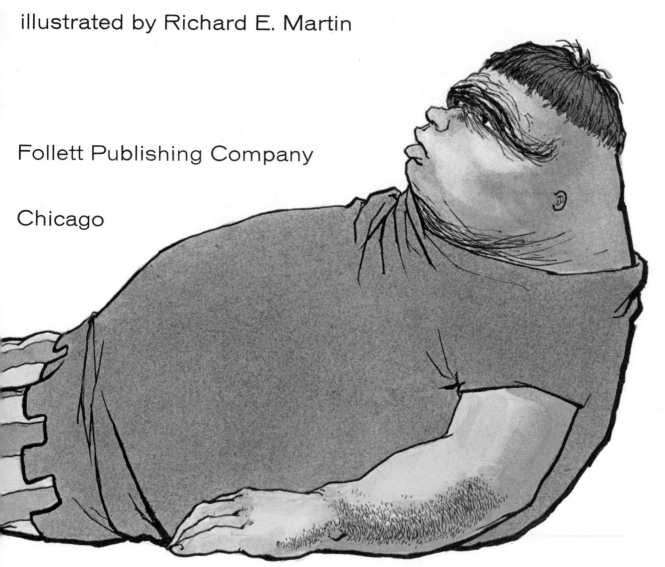

Library of Congress Catalog Card Number: 64-15631

EYOND high mountains and deep in a forest there was once a house in the shape of a big crystal ball. In the crystal ball house lived a large family of magicians. There was the father magician, who always wore a high, pointed red hat and a long blue cape lined with red silk. There was the mother magician, who always wore a high, pointed blue hat and a long red cape lined with blue silk. And there were their many, many children, who, as soon as they learned to do magic spells, also wore magic hats and capes. Only the smallest and youngest child, little Arthur—or Arfur, as he called himself—didn't wear magic clothes. He wore just plain pants because he didn't know any magic.

It was a busy family, for there was a lot of work to do. Some of the older children who had learned to fly polished the outside of the crystal ball house. The other children sharpened magic wands, tended the box of magic tricks, and polished the family's magic mirror. But not little Arthur. Since the rest of the family used magic to get the work done, he could only watch and wish that he, too, could help.

All day long the mother and father magicians were busy playing magic tricks on a giant called Thundermouth, who, with his wicked pet parrot, lived in a nearby castle.

Thundermouth, with the parrot perched on his head, roamed the countryside searching out victims for his terrible weapon—a tongue that he could snap like a whip.

The thundering crack it made when it snapped caused everyone who heard it to stand stock still in fright. And then Thundermouth would capture someone—often a princess.

It was the magicians' tricks that kept the people who lived in the countryside safe from the giant's tongue, but it was tiring work.

One evening, when the father and mother magicians returned from a particularly hard day, Arthur pleaded, "Muvver, don't you fink I could learn some magic, too?"

His mother didn't answer. Instead she waved her hands and said:

Thittery Thattery Thoom.
Let me have my broom.

And whoosh! A broom appeared in her hands and she began to sweep.

Arthur pleaded again. "Please, Muvver! Can't I have a cape, too? I fink I can learn one little magic spell."

His mother stopped sweeping. "Now Arthur, it's no use begging. I told you before that if you aren't old enough to talk right you aren't old enough to say magic spells. Call your brothers and sisters for supper. Your father and I are looking forward to an evening of peace and quiet, with no trouble from you children or that nasty Thundermouth."

When everyone was seated at the table, the mother magician waved her hands and said:

Thittery Thattery Thilk.
Everyone has some milk.

Whoosh! A glass of milk appeared at each person's place.

Thittery Thattery Thinach.
Everyone has some spinach.

Whoosh again! Spinach appeared.

"I'm not going to eat this old supper," whispered one of the older children. "I'm going to make my own."

Thittery Thattery Thandy.
Let me have some candy.

And there before him was a large plate of chocolates. Arthur wanted to try, too:

Fittery Fattery Fake.
Let me have some cake.

13

Of course, nothing happened, so Arthur tried again:

> Sittery Sattery. . . .
> Tittery Tattery. . . .

But no matter how hard he tried, Arthur just couldn't say the magic spell.

"That is quite enough, children," said the father magician sternly. "You know you aren't allowed to use magic to get dessert before you eat your spinach and drink your milk. As punishment, you are to wash these dishes instead of making them disappear."

But just at that moment the magic mirror began to shake and jangle and change color.

"Someone is finking of us! Someone is calling us!" cried Arthur.

"Yes? Yes? Who is it?" asked the father magician.

Slowly a picture began to form in the mirror. There in the dungeon in the giant's castle sat Thundermouth, holding a huge birdcage. In it was a beautiful princess, with her long, golden hair tied tightly across her mouth so that she couldn't speak.

"Anovver princess has been captured by Fundermouf!" cried Arthur.

"Oh, no! Not again!" sighed the mother magician.

"Yes, my dear. I'm afraid it's Princess Goldenhair. We must go to her rescue immediately," said the father wearily.

"We want to go, too! We want to go, too!" shouted all the children at once.

"Very well. You may all come," the father said.

"Hooray! Fank you!" cheered Arthur, as he ran for the door.

"Except Arthur," said his mother firmly. "You are too little to go out at night, and since you can't say any of the magic spells, you won't be any help at all. But as a special treat, you may shine some stars while we are gone."

Poor Arthur! He was home all alone while everyone else went off to rescue the princess from the wicked giant. He kicked sadly at the pile of stars waiting to be polished. He was so unhappy that he decided to ask the magic mirror a question—something that was done only in an emergency.

"Magic mirror, magic mirror, I have a question to ask you," said little Arthur in a trembly voice.

The mirror clouded over and the lights in the crystal ball house became dim. Out of the mirror came a deep voice, saying slowly:

> I will do any task.
> What is it you ask?

"Oh, mirror," begged Arthur, "how can I learn to say magic spells?"

The mirror gulped and blew out a billow of smoke.

> Arthur, your mother firmly says "No."
> Is it to the trash heap you want me to go?

"Just one little hint? Please!" begged Arthur.

The mirror was silent for a moment. Then it said swiftly:

> Here's one hint that you must know.
> Just put it out and then you blow.

"Put what out?" cried Arthur, as the lights became bright again and the mirror cleared. "I don't understand. Come back!"

But instead the mirror started to jangle and shake and change color.

"Someone is finking of me! Someone is calling me!"
Arthur cried, watching the picture form. He could plainly
see the dungeon again and Thundermouth with his awful
parrot on his head. In the birdcage were not only Princess
Goldenhair, but also Arthur's mother and father and sisters
and brothers! They all had their capes tied across their
mouths so that not a single one could say a magic spell
to save them.

"Fundermouf has captured everyone!" gasped Arthur.
"Oh, if I could only say a magic spell!" He thought of
the mirror's riddle:

> Here's one hint that you must know.
> Just put it out and then you blow.

Arthur tried putting out his foot and blowing, but all
he was able to say was "Tittery Tattery. . . ."

He tried turning his pockets inside out and blowing, but all he said was "Fittery Fattery . . . Sittery Sattery. . . ."

"I don't know *what* to put out. I must go to Fundermouf's castle and rescue everyone by myself!" he decided bravely.

He plunged into the dark woods. The branches of the trees tore his clothes and the owls hooted. Arthur felt that there was danger everywhere. On he ran, thinking only of the task ahead.

At last he reached Thundermouth's castle. Down into
the dungeon he raced as he heard the giant roaring,
"Ho-ho-ho! You can't sing your magic any longer, can you,
my little birds?"

"Little birds!" echoed the parrot.

In burst Arthur, shouting, "You let my family go—you
mean old giant you!" And he kicked and struck hard at
the giant's knee, which was as high as he could reach.

"What have we here?" asked Thundermouth, as he put
down the cage to see what was tickling his knee. "What?
Another pretty bird for my birdcage?" He reached down to
pick Arthur up.

"Put it out! Put it out!" cackled the wicked parrot,
urging Thundermouth to snap his terrible tongue.

Arthur watched in horror as the giant began to curl up
his tongue so that he could snap it with a thundering crack.

"Put it out? Put it out?" Arthur suddenly understood what the mirror had told him. It was his *tongue* he must put out. Then he must blow. Quick as a wink he did just that, shouting, "Th-Th-Thundermouth-th, you are th-th-through!"

> Thittery Thattery Tho.
> I want this giant and parrot to go.

And with the biggest whooooosh of all, Thundermouth and the parrot disappeared, never to be heard from again.

Again Arthur tried a magic spell:

> Thittery Thattery Thee.
> Let everyone go free!

Whoosh again! There stood an empty cage. There were Arthur's whole family and the princess, hugging and kissing him and dancing around him in joy.

The beautiful princess smiled at him gratefully and said, "My father, the king, will reward you with anything you wish, little Arthur."

"But," said Arthur, "all I want in the world is to wear a high pointed hat and a long blue cape lined with red silk and to be able to help with the magic spells."

So Arthur was taken triumphantly home by his proud family and was given a tall, tall hat and a long, long cape.

Soon he was the finest magician of them all.

THE LISTEN-HEAR BOOKS

The Listen-Hear books provide teachers and parents with an entertaining and simple method of speech improvement for children in kindergarten and the early primary grades. The books also provide imaginative and enjoyable stories.

The books were written especially for the child who has an auditory discrimination problem and needs ear training but who has normal hearing and does not have a speech defect—the child who says *wed*, for instance, and thinks he is saying *red*. The stories and illustrations are so imaginative, however, that all children enjoy them. The stories also help all children develop good speaking habits, which in turn help develop good reading habits.

The books are ideal for read-aloud time. The *Teacher's Guide* for the set of six books provides instructions for games that the children can play after they have heard each story. The games give children practice in listening, hearing, and making the correct sounds.

Each book deals with one sound that many children find difficult to make:

> The Roaring Dragon of Redrose—for the sound of *R*
> Magic Arthur and the Giant—for the sound of *Th*
> Mr. Sipple and the Naughty Princess—for the sound of *S*
> The Cock Who Couldn't Crow—for the sound of *K*
> Alfie and the Dream Machine—for the sound of *F*
> Lester and the Sea Monster—for the sound of *L*

The authors, Jan Slepian and Ann Seidler, have each had more than ten years experience in speech therapy.

Mrs. Slepian has been a speech therapist at the Language Clinic at Massachusetts General Hospital in Boston and the National Hospital for Speech Disorders in New York.

Mrs. Seidler has been a speech therapist at the National Hospital for Speech Disorders in New York and speech consultant for the public schools of Cedar Grove, New Jersey.

Both authors are members of the American Speech and Hearing Association and the New Jersey Speech and Hearing Association.